Ant-Man and the Wasp Save the Day!

DK | Penguin Random House

Editors Vicky Armstrong and Julia March
Project Art Editor Stefan Georgiou
Senior Production Editor Jennifer Murray
Senior Production Controller Mary Slater
Managing Editor Emma Grange
Managing Art Editor Vicky Short
Publishing Director Mark Searle

Reading Consultant Barbara Marinak

First American Edition, 2023
Published in the United States by DK Publishing
1745 Broadway, 20th Floor, New York, NY 10019

DK, a Division of Penguin Random House LLC
23 24 25 26 27 10 9 8 7 6 5 4 3 2 1
001-332601-Feb/23

Published in Great Britain by Dorling Kindersley Limited

A catalog record for this book
is available from the Library of Congress.
ISBN: 978-0-7440-7987-6 (Paperback)
ISBN: 978-0-7440-7988-3 (Hardcover)

DK books are available at special discounts when purchased in bulk
for sales promotions, premiums, fund-raising, or educational use.
For details, contact: DK Publishing Special Markets,
1745 Broadway, 20th Floor, New York, NY 10019
SpecialSales@dk.com

Printed and bound in China

For the curious
www.dk.com

MIX
Paper | Supporting responsible forestry
FSC www.fsc.org FSC™ C018179

This book was made with Forest Stewardship Council ™ certified paper - one small step in DK's commitment to a sustainable future.
For more information go to www.dk.com/our-green-pledge

Level 3

Ant-Man and the Wasp Save the Day!

Written by Julia March

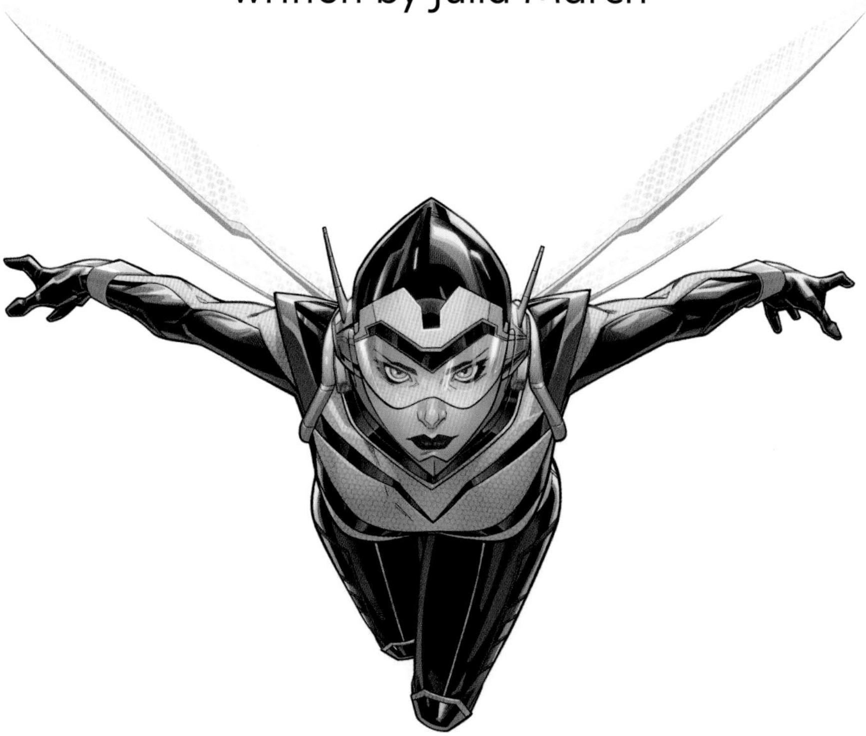

DK

Contents

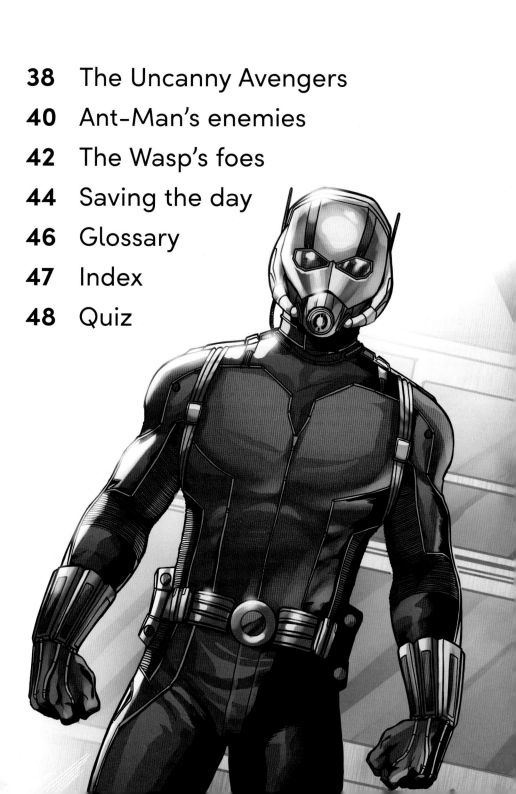

Meet Ant-Man

Scott Lang is the Super Hero known as Ant-Man. He gets his name because he commands an army of ants. He can shrink to ant size, too. In fact, he can sometimes make himself even smaller. And all without losing any of his strength!

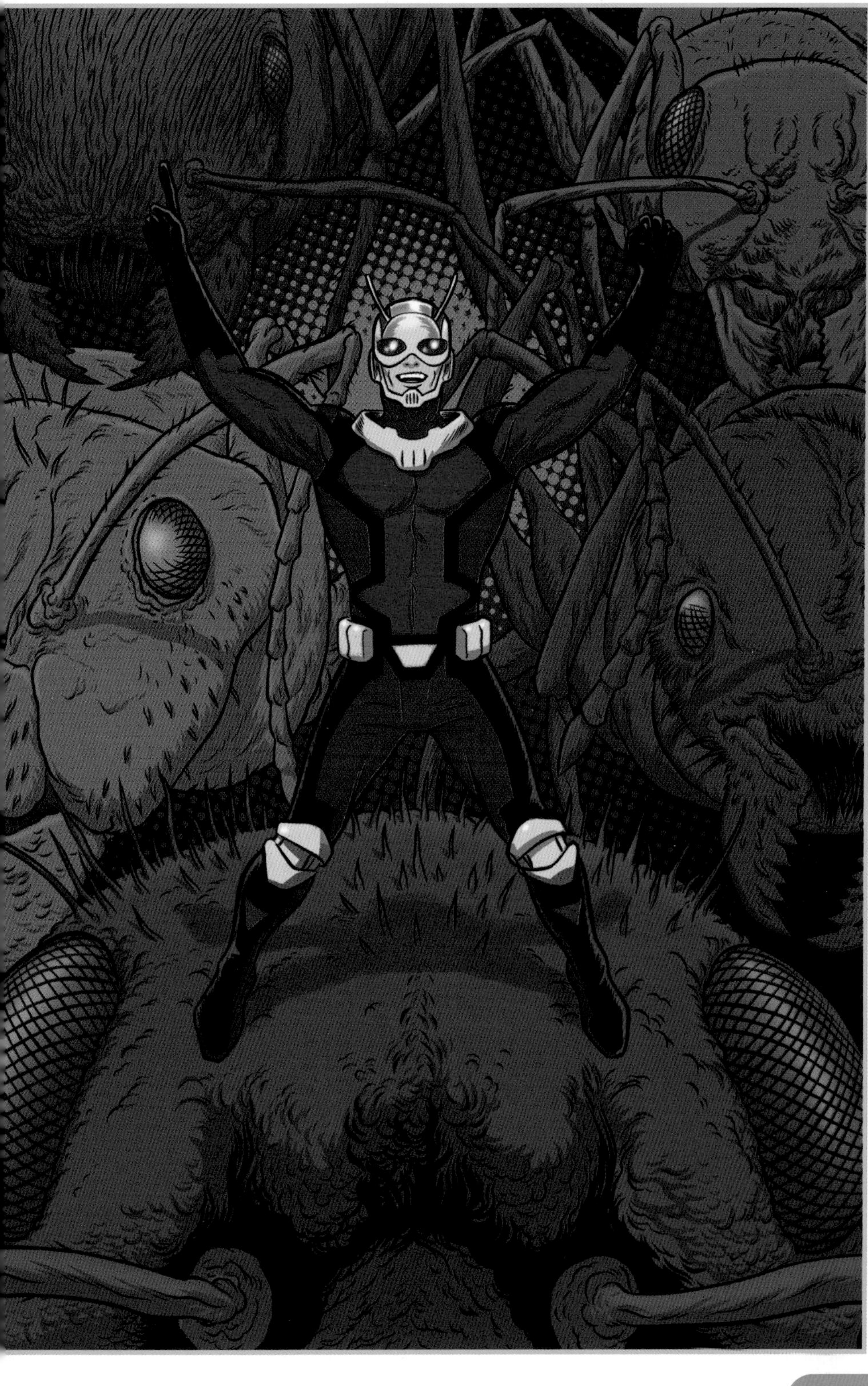

Meet the Wasp

Janet Van Dyne is another Super Hero who can shrink. She named herself the Wasp because she has wings and wears stingers on her wrists. The Wasp is a cheerful, friendly person. She is even quite kind to her foes if they are sorry.

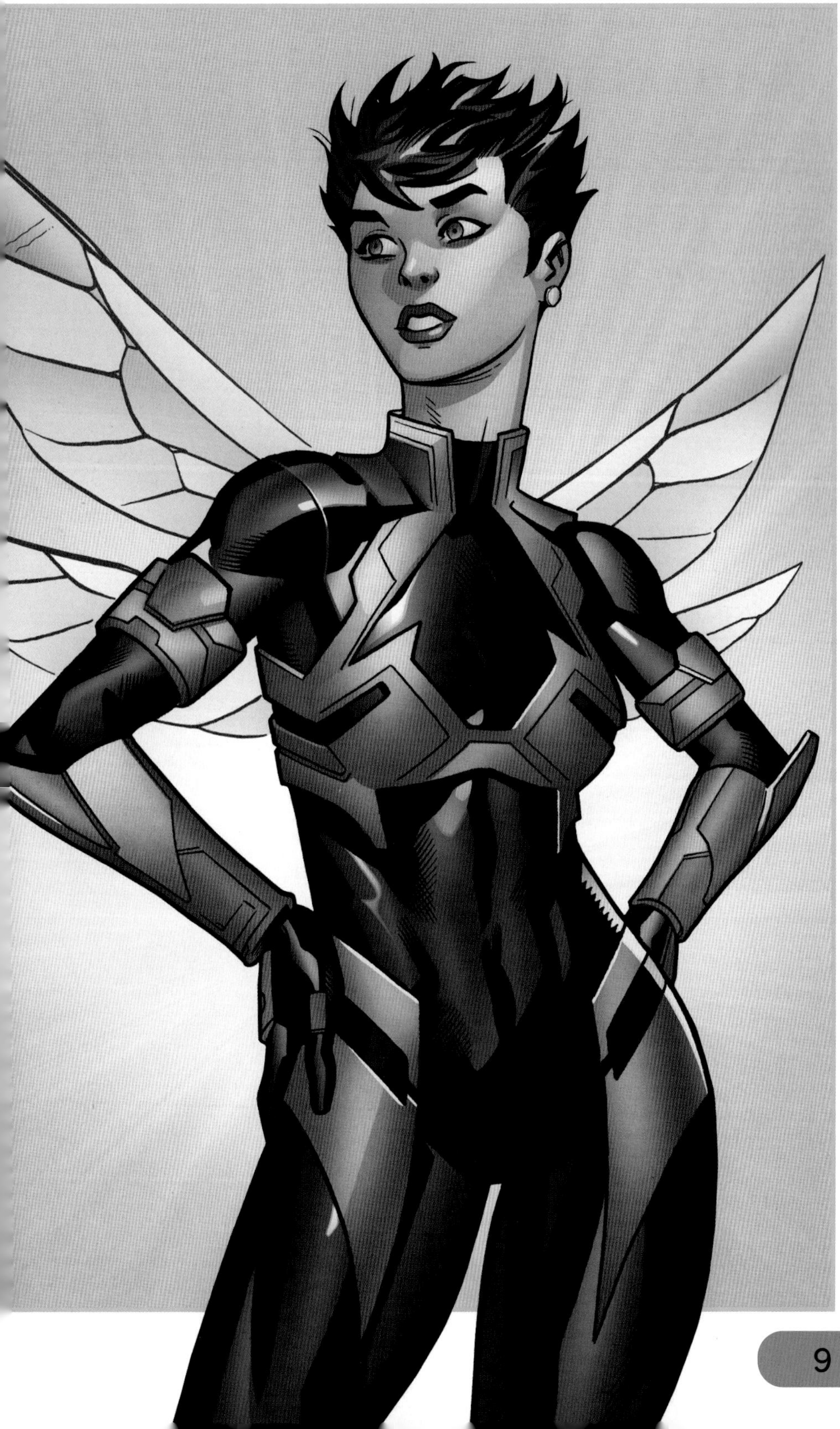

Super friends

Ant-Man and the Wasp are good friends. They met when Ant-Man joined a mission to rescue the Wasp. She had gone missing while tracking down a criminal doctor. Together, Ant-Man and the Wasp defeated the doctor.

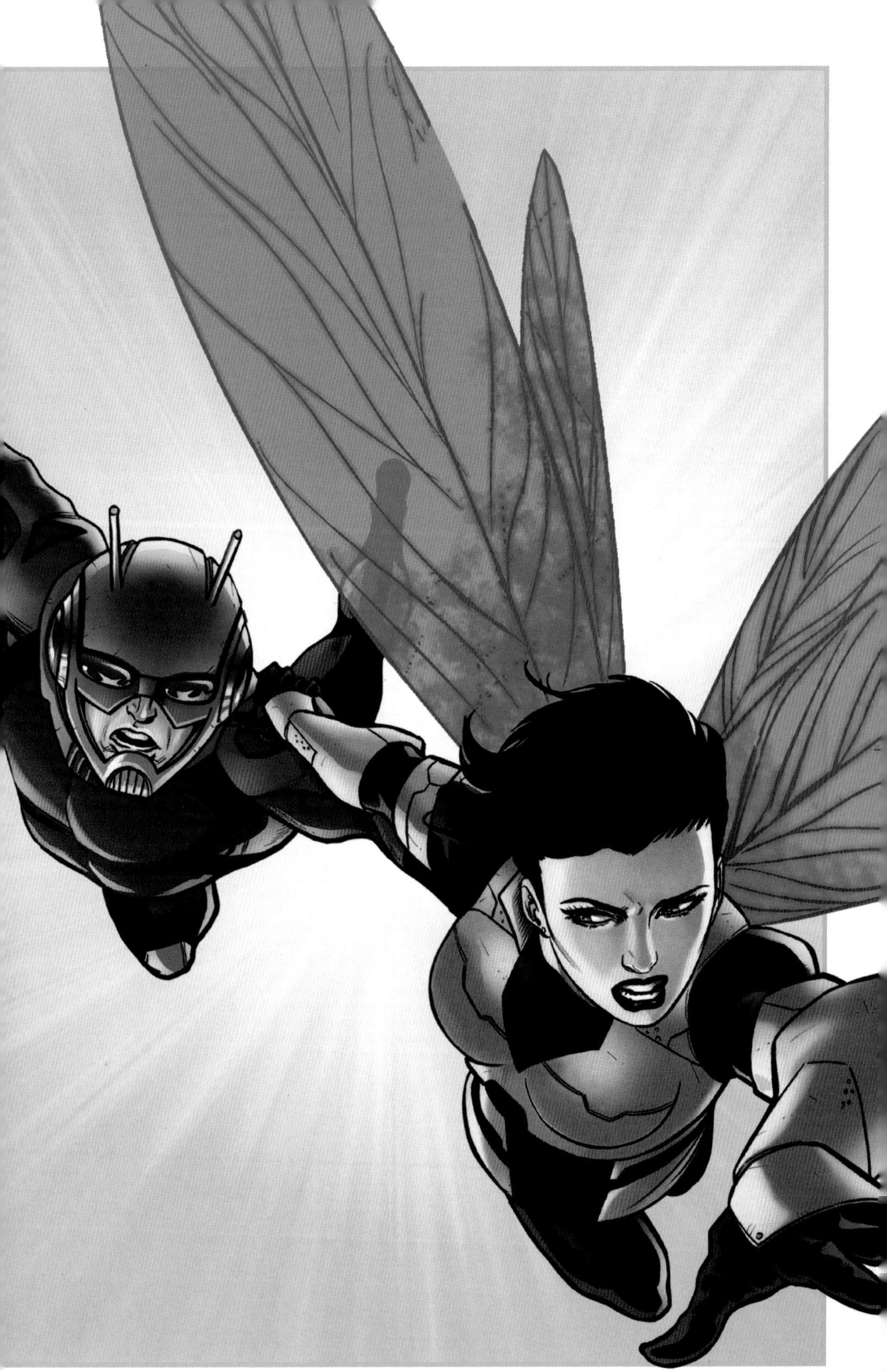

Becoming Ant-Man

Scott was given his Ant-Man suit by a scientist named Hank Pym. Hank knew Scott had worked hard to leave a life of crime and become an electrical engineer. He thought Scott would make a great Super Hero. And he was right!

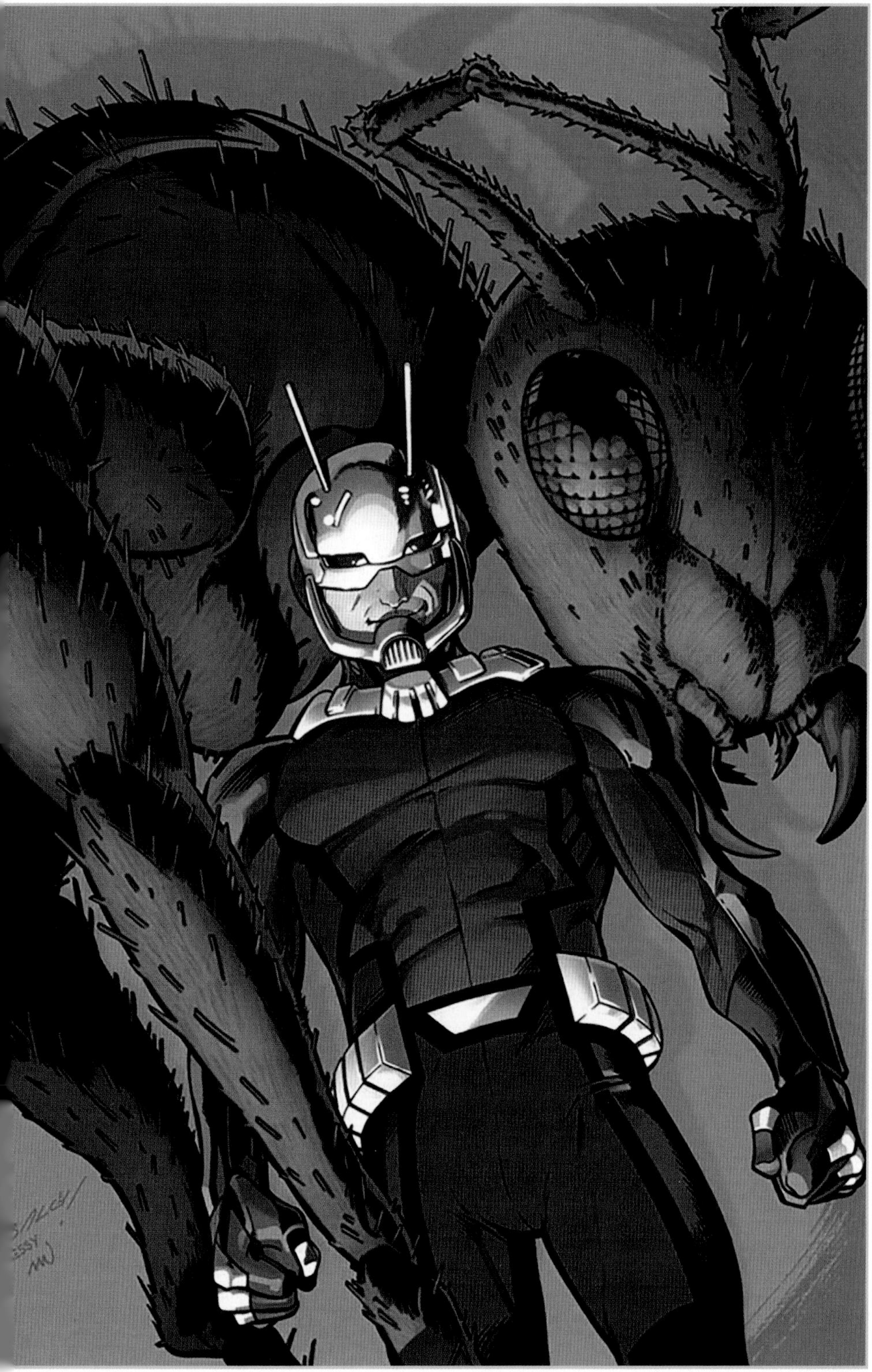

The first Ant-Man

Scott Lang is not the only hero to wear the Ant-Man suit. Hank Pym was the first Ant-Man. He invented a suit that could make him shrink or grow. The secret was something he called Pym Particles.

Scott Lang

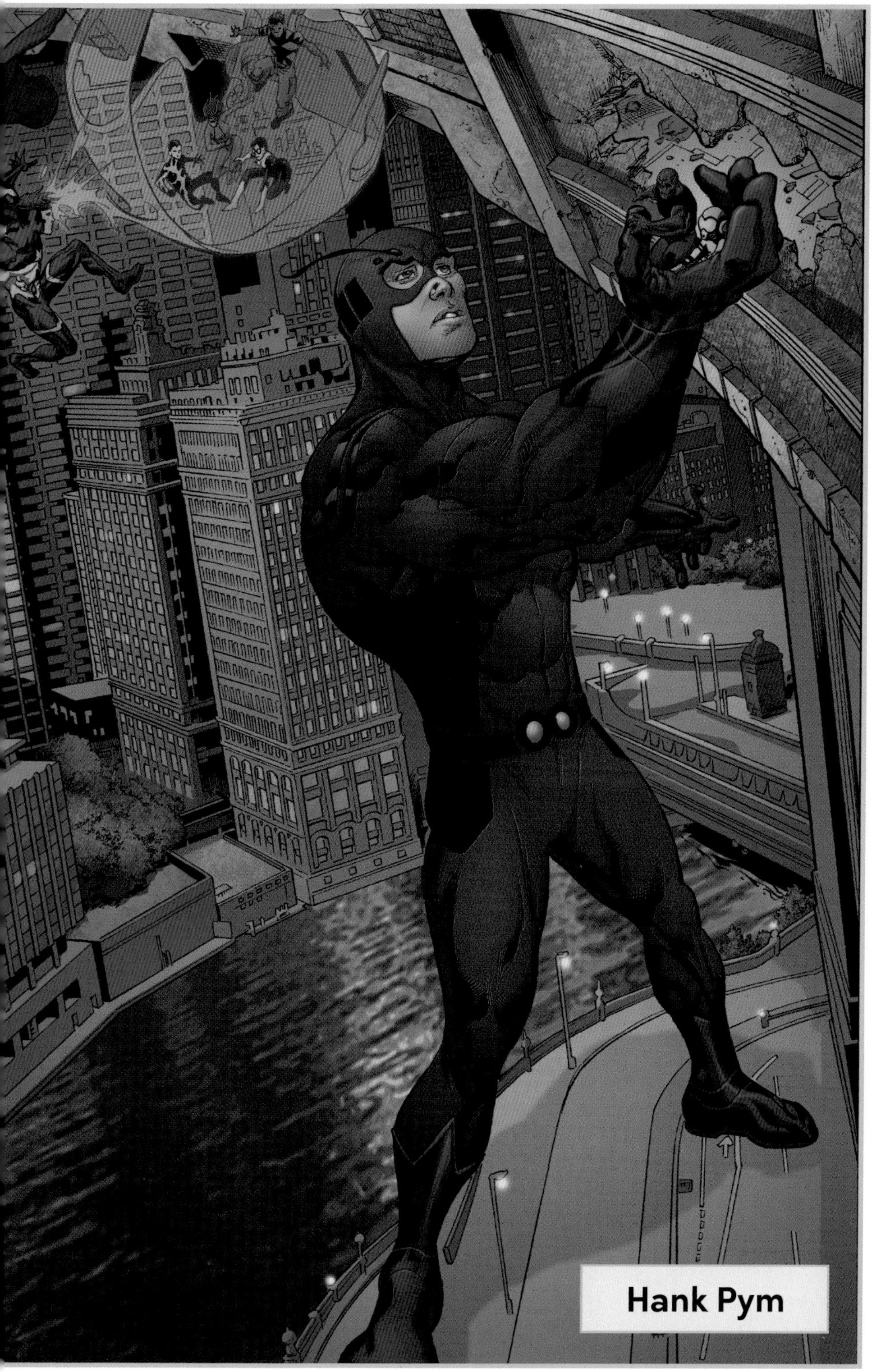
Hank Pym

Becoming the Wasp

When an alien monster killed her father, Janet Van Dyne wanted revenge. She went to Hank Pym for help. He made Janet a fantastic Wasp suit with wings and stingers. The alien was soon made to buzz off!

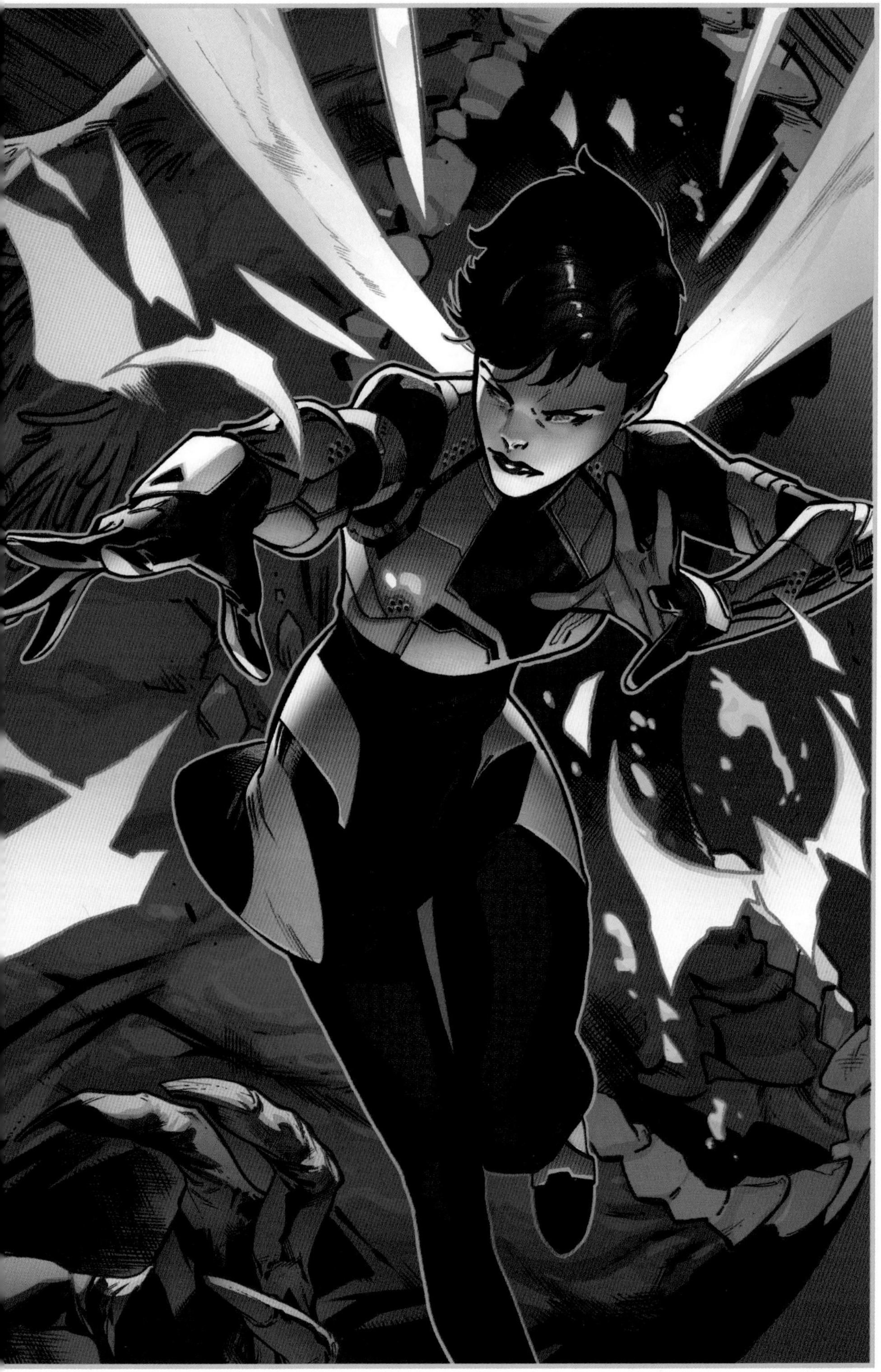

Other Wasps

Janet sometimes lets others take over as the Wasp. Hank Pym briefly became the Wasp when Janet was stuck in a tiny world called the Underverse. Janet now shares the role of the Wasp with her stepdaughter, Nadia. Nadia is brave, caring, and very, very clever.

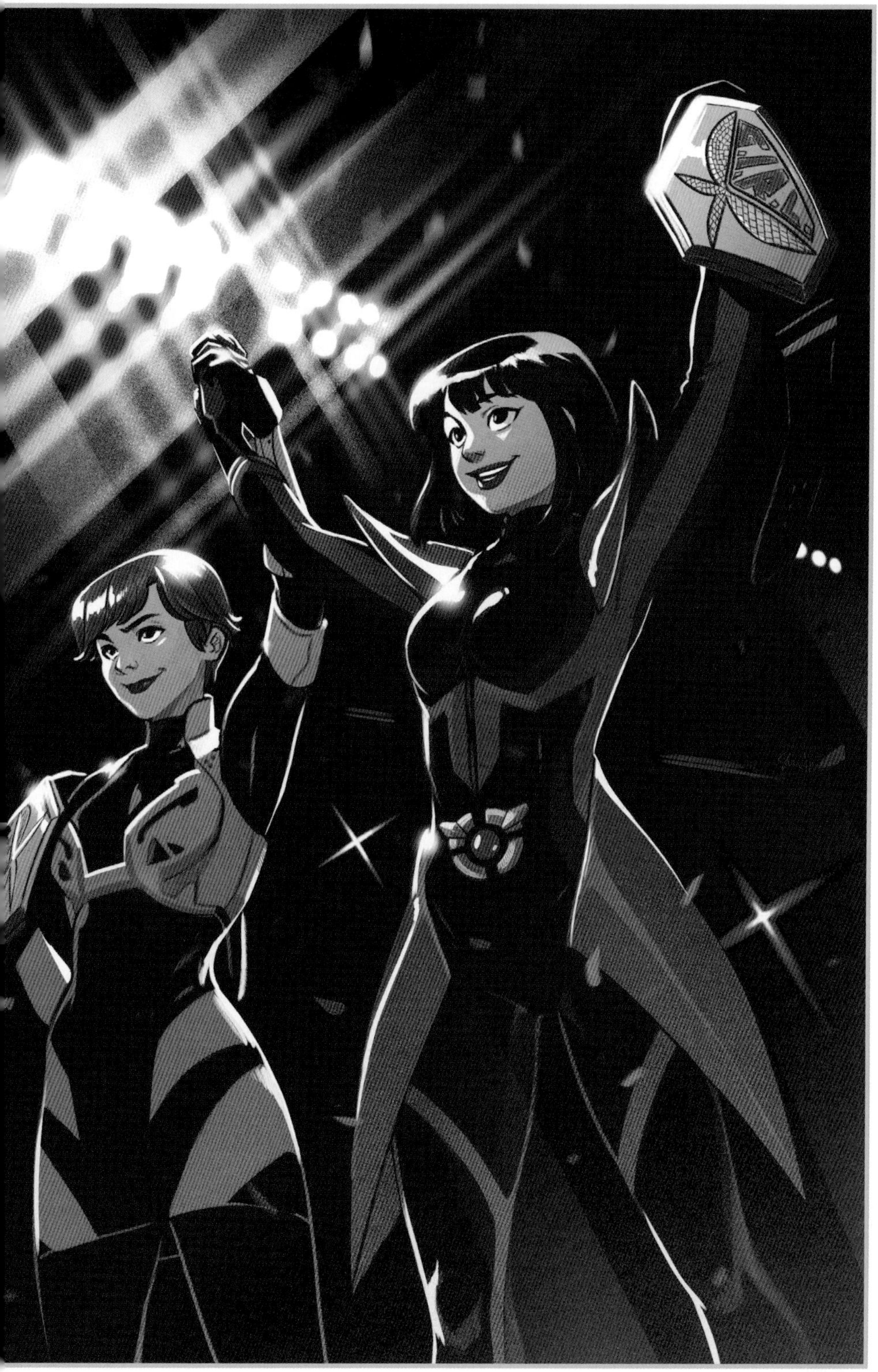

G.I.R.L.

Janet is a great role model for Nadia. Nadia wants to encourage other girls to aim high, just like the two of them. She has started a program to find the world's most brilliant women. It is called G.I.R.L. That stands for Geniuses In action Research Labs.

**Geniuses In action
Research Labs**

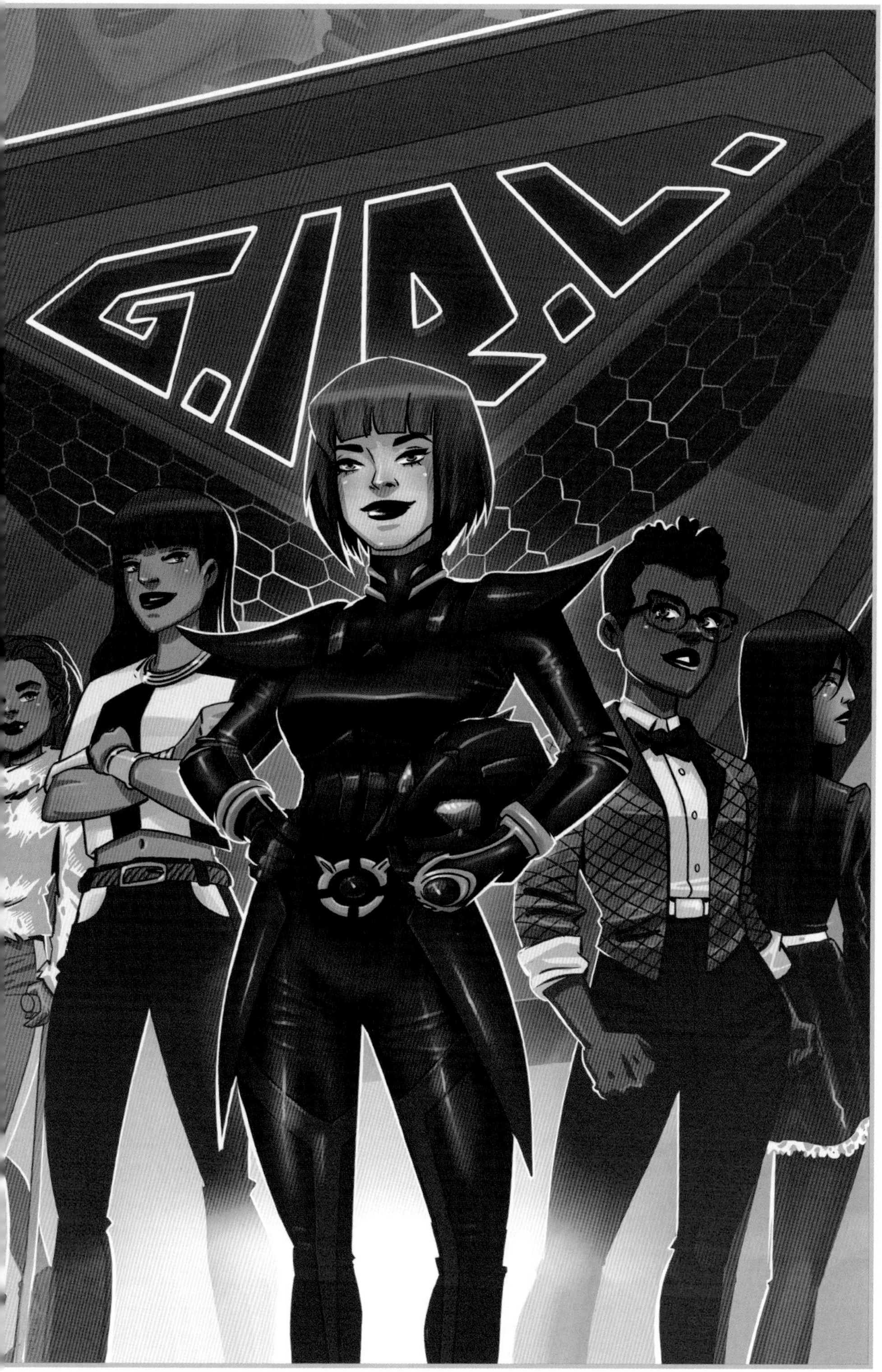
G.I.R.L.

Amazing powers

There is no danger of Ant-Man or the Wasp being squashed. When they shrink, they keep their full-size strength. They can grow to giant size, too. And they can control insects with their minds. These powers are all due to the amazing Pym Particles in their suits.

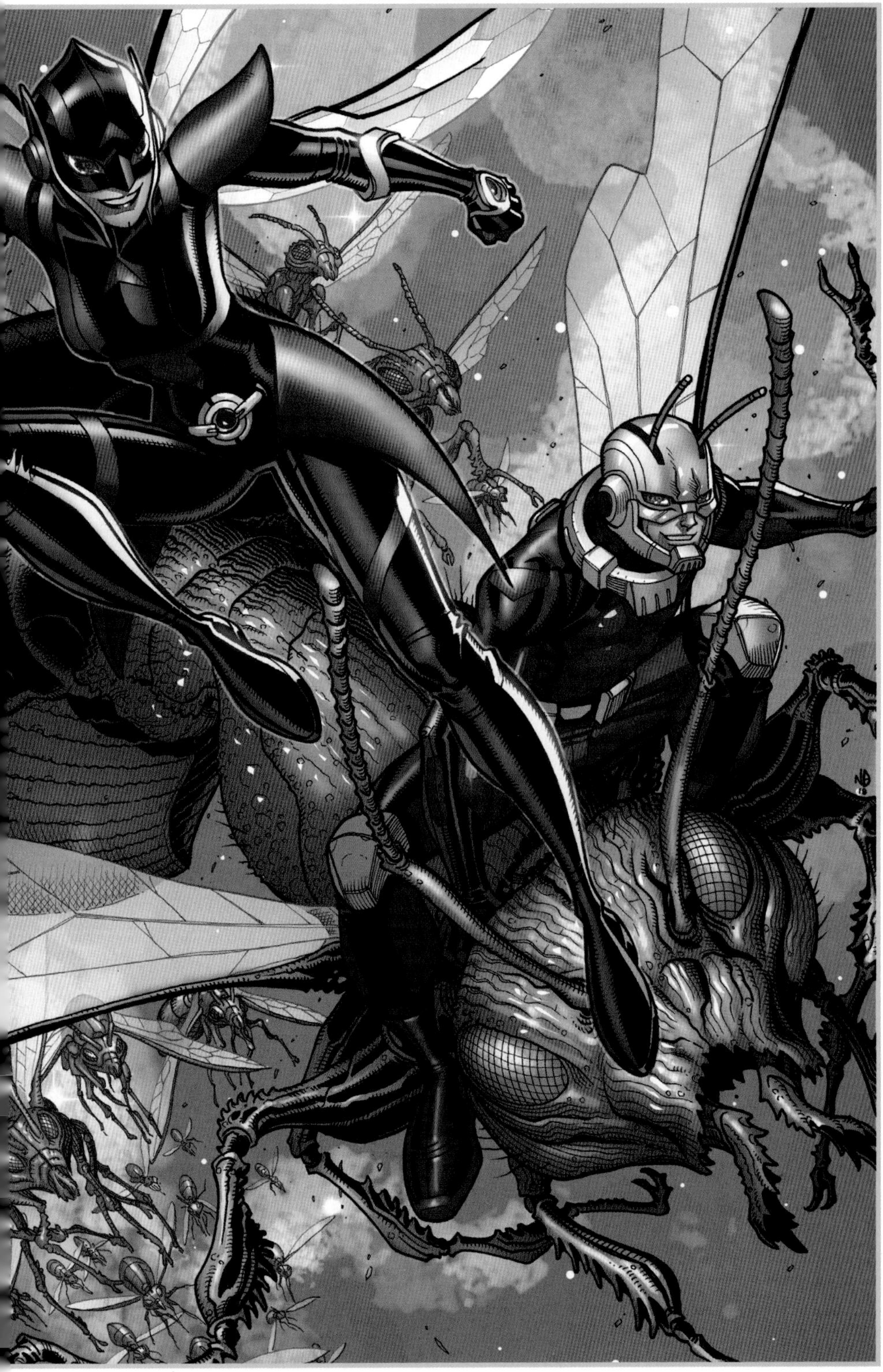

Ant-Man Super Hero suit

Ant-Man has made changes to his suit over time. Here are some of its features.

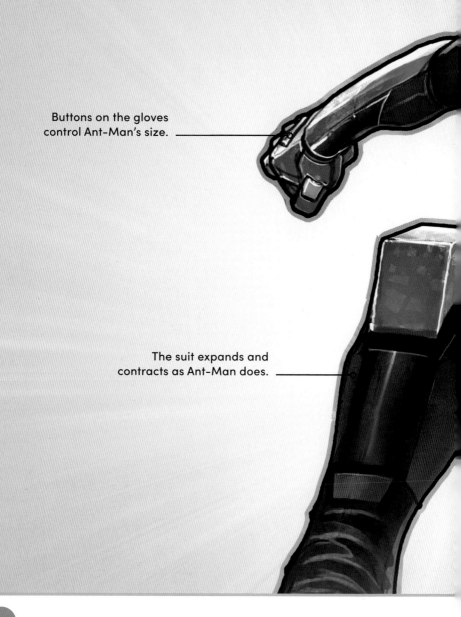

Buttons on the gloves control Ant-Man's size.

The suit expands and contracts as Ant-Man does.

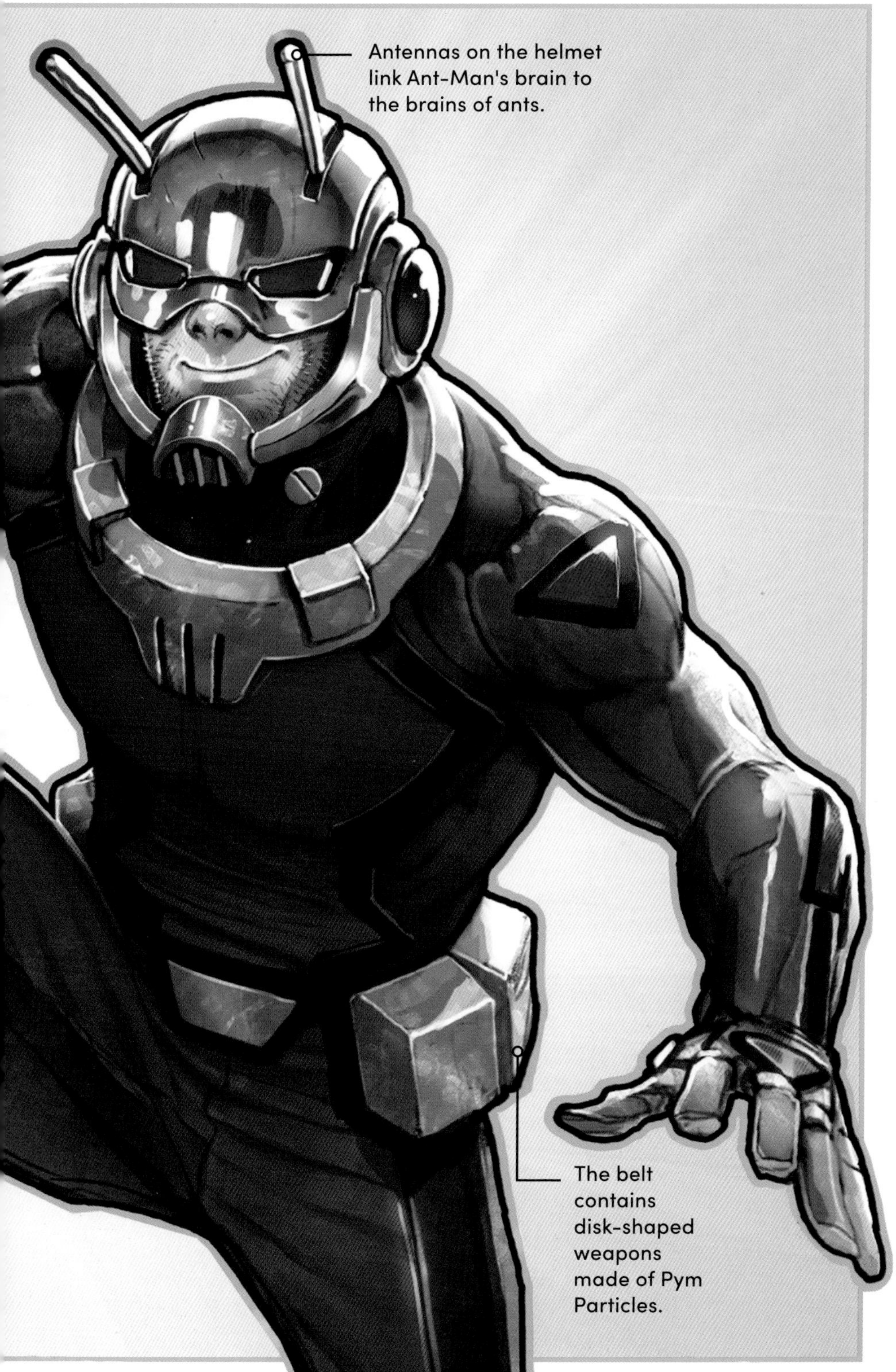
Antennas on the helmet link Ant-Man's brain to the brains of ants.
The belt contains disk-shaped weapons made of Pym Particles.

The Wasp Super Hero suit

Janet used to be a fashion designer. She uses her skills to update her suit often.

The wings are made from fabric created in a lab.

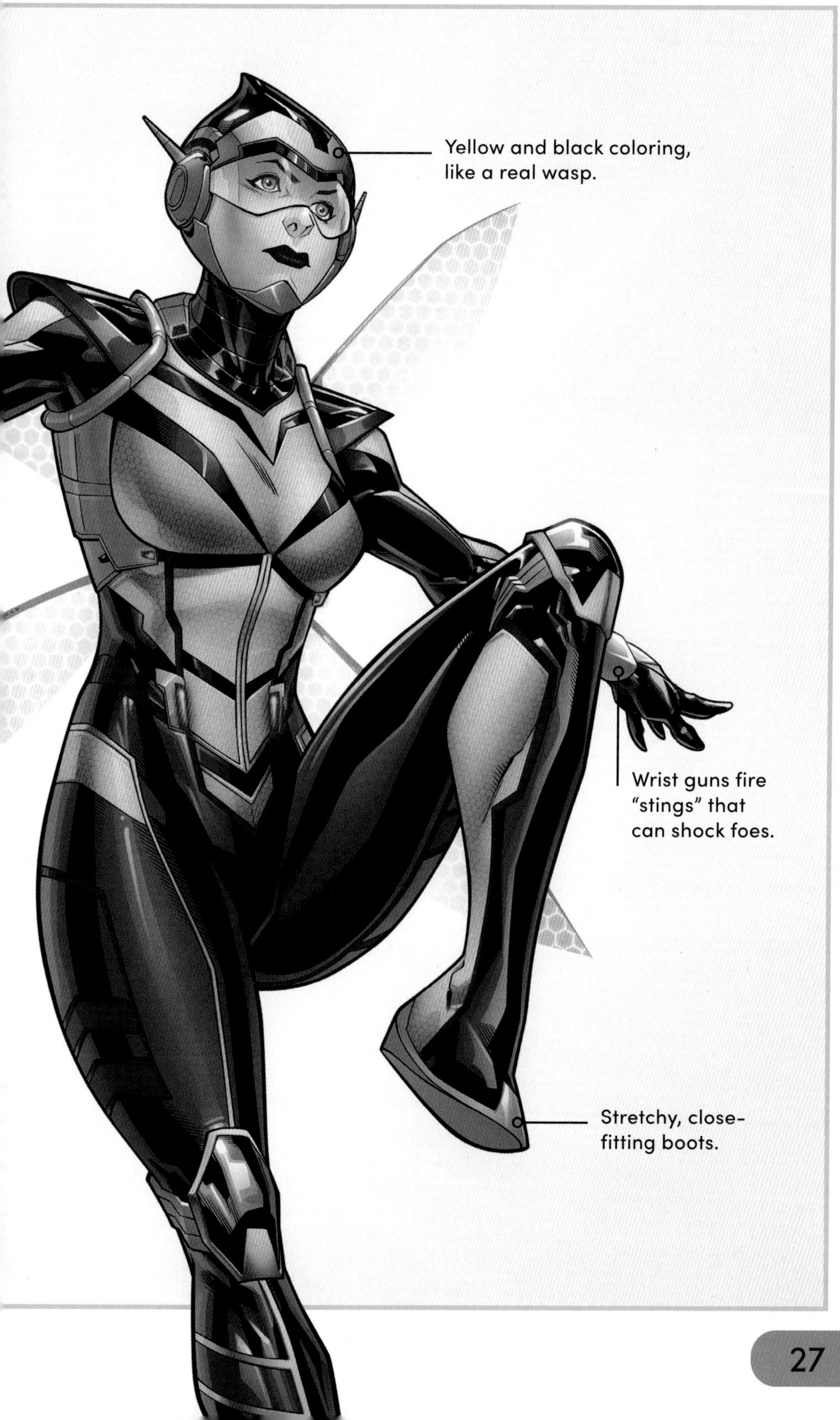
Yellow and black coloring, like a real wasp.
Wrist guns fire "stings" that can shock foes.
Stretchy, close-fitting boots.

Ant army

Ant-Man does not use his voice to talk to his ant army. He can connect his brain directly to theirs so they know what he wants them to do. When he is riding an ant into battle, Ant-Man does not even need reins to steer.

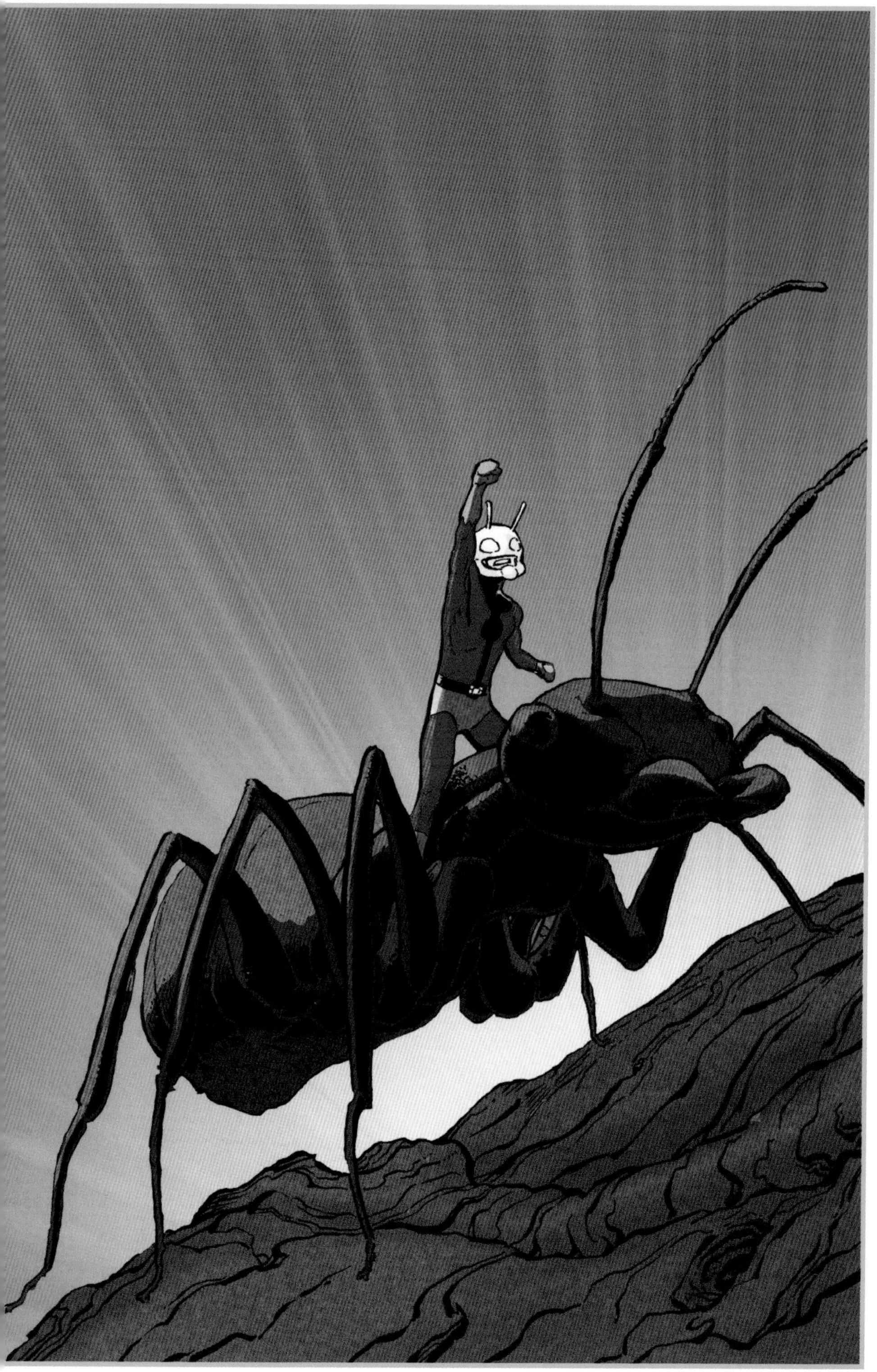

Across the Universe

If there is an emergency in the Universe, Ant-Man and the Wasp will be there. Between them they have defeated robots, aliens, and super villains. They have even battled foes in a strange place called the Quantum Realm. And every time, they have saved the day!

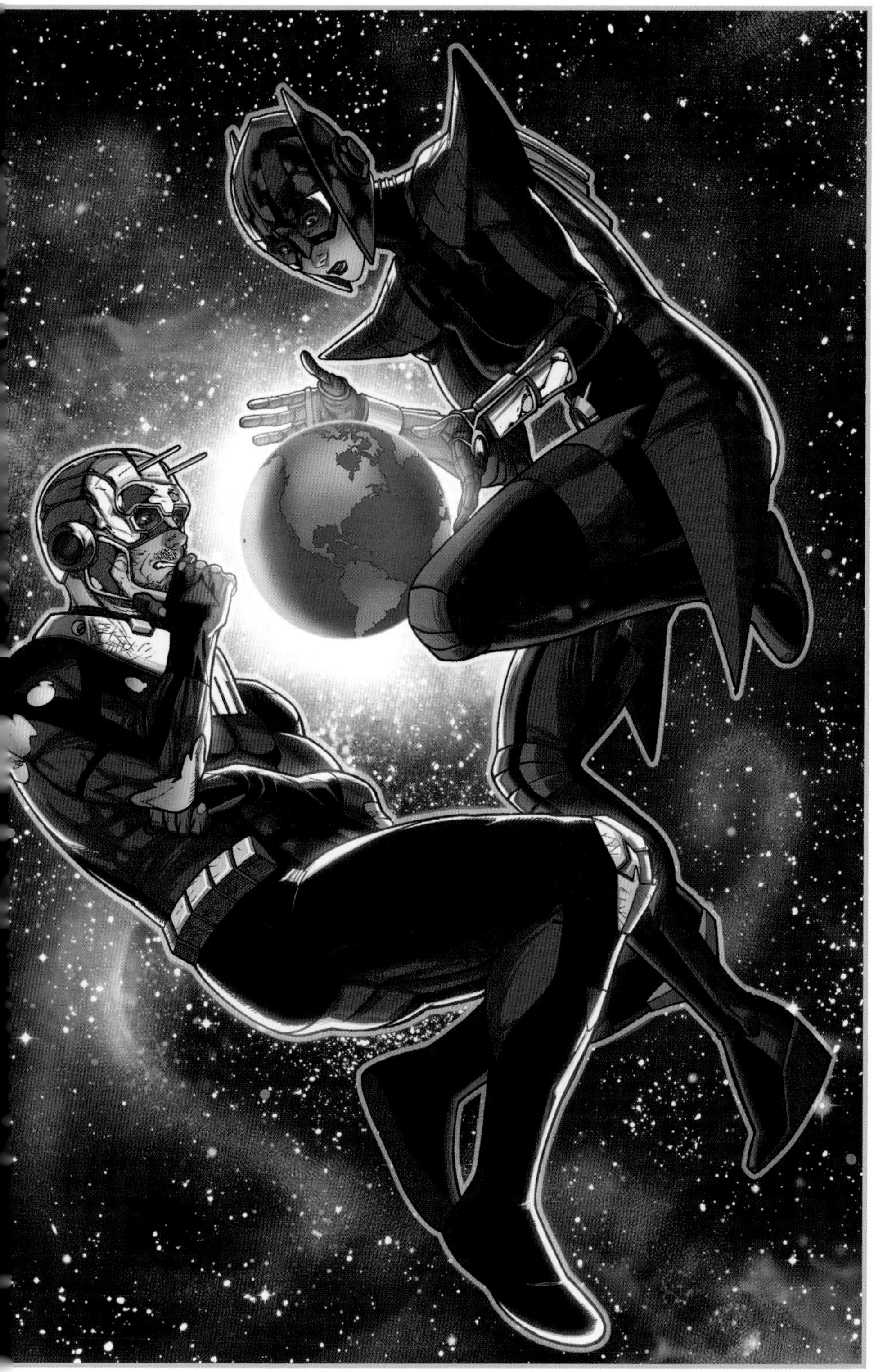

Team players

Super Heroes often combine as teams. Ant-Man has been in the Guardians of the Galaxy, the Fantastic Four, and the Future Foundation. The Wasp has been in the Uncanny Avengers and the Defenders. Ant-Man and the Wasp have both been members of The Avengers.

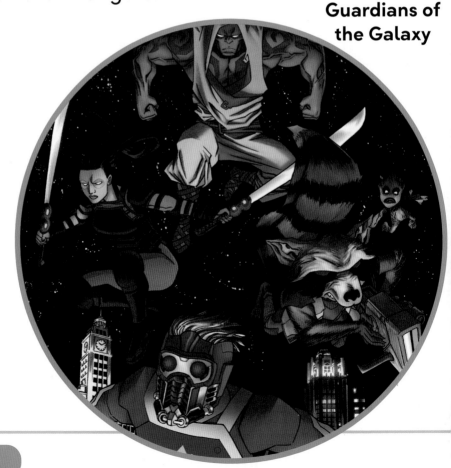

Guardians of the Galaxy

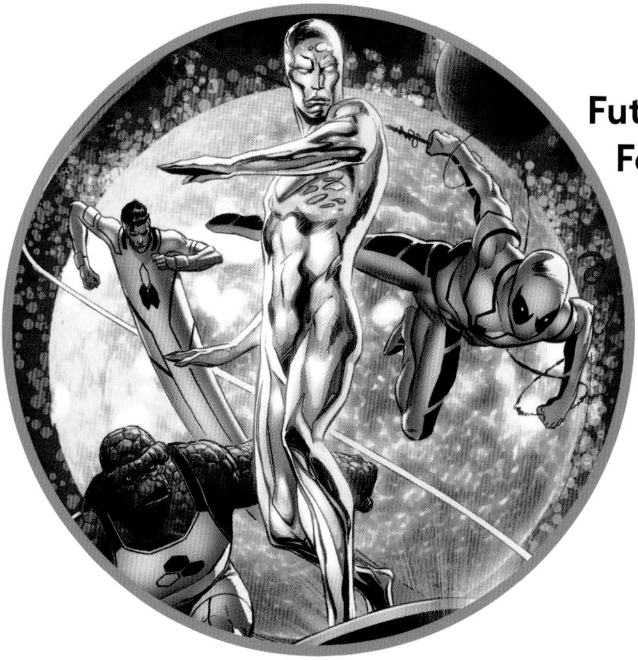

Future Foundation

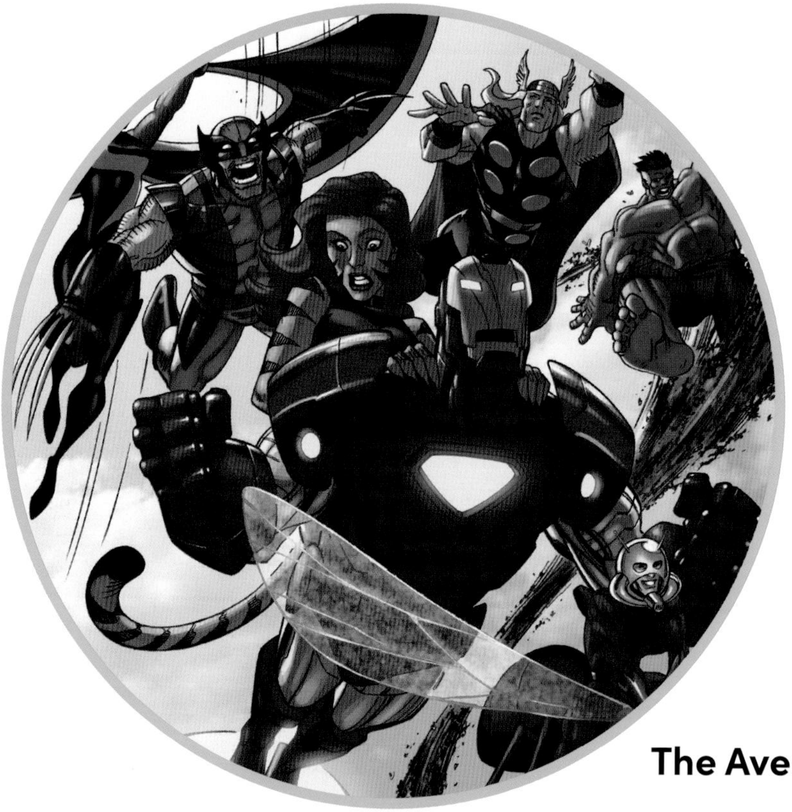

The Avengers

The Avengers

The Avengers are Earth's mightiest Super Heroes. Ant-Man and the Wasp have both been members of this famous team. The Wasp thought up their name, and even led the team for a while. Her warmth and patience made her a very popular leader.

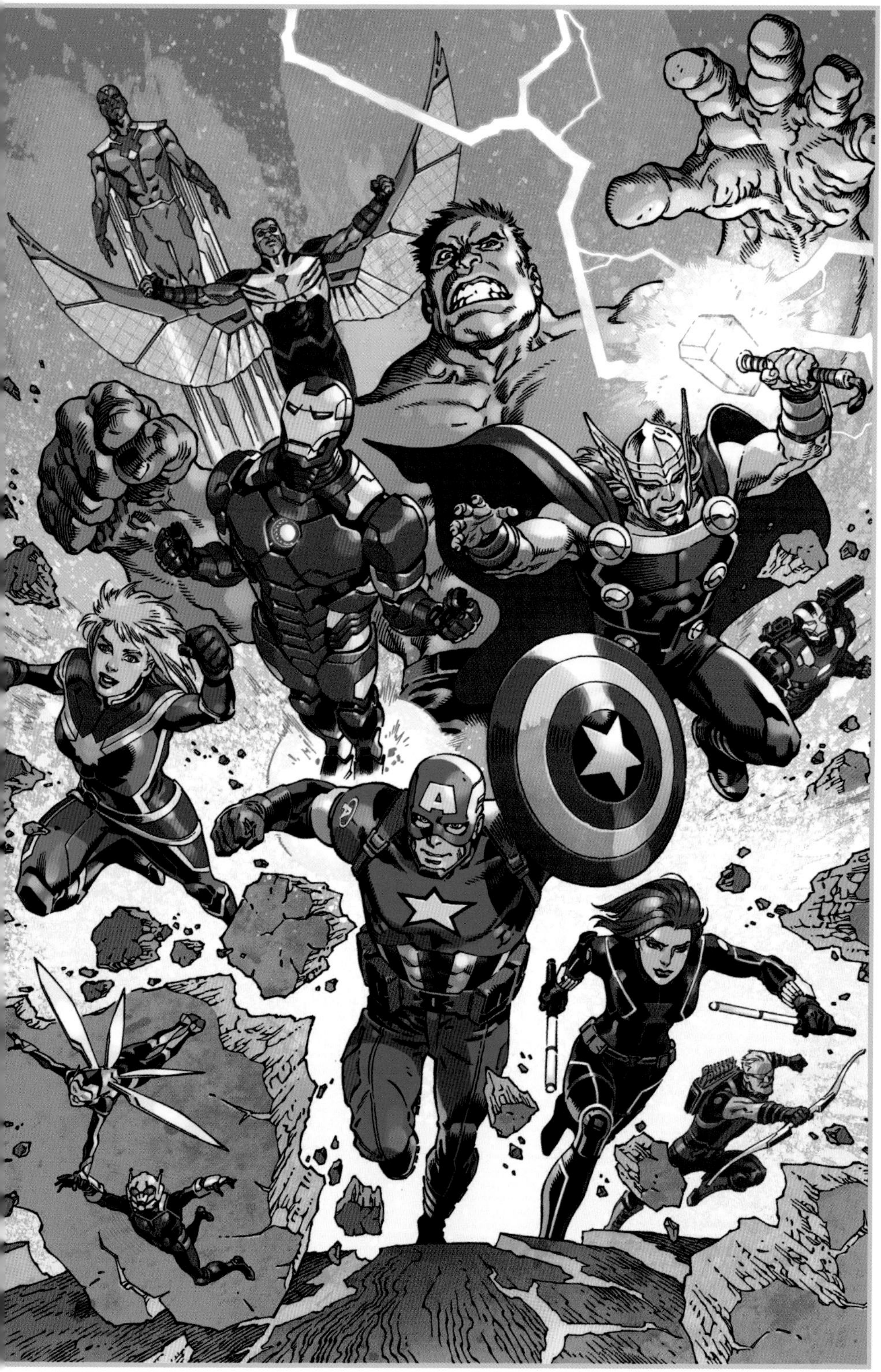

The Fantastic Four

The Fantastic Four are a famous Super Hero team made up of Mr. Fantastic, the Invisible Woman, the Human Torch, and the Thing. Sometimes, one of the team goes missing during an adventure. When that happens, Ant-Man often steps in to save the day.

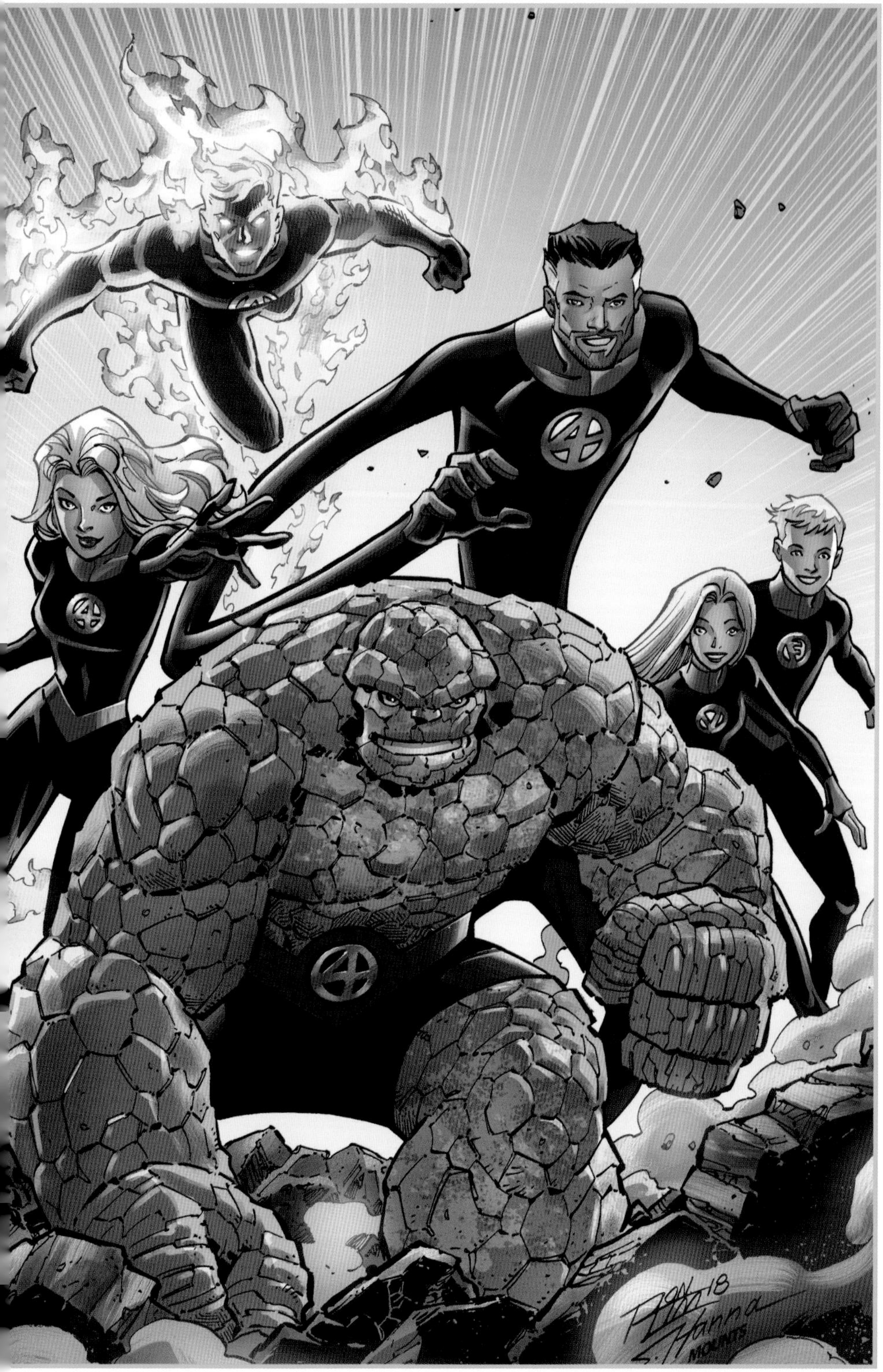

The Uncanny Avengers

The Uncanny Avengers are a Super Hero team made up of humans and mutants. The Wasp was happy to join this mixed team. She thinks human and mutant Super Heroes should work together in harmony. After all, they are all on the same side.

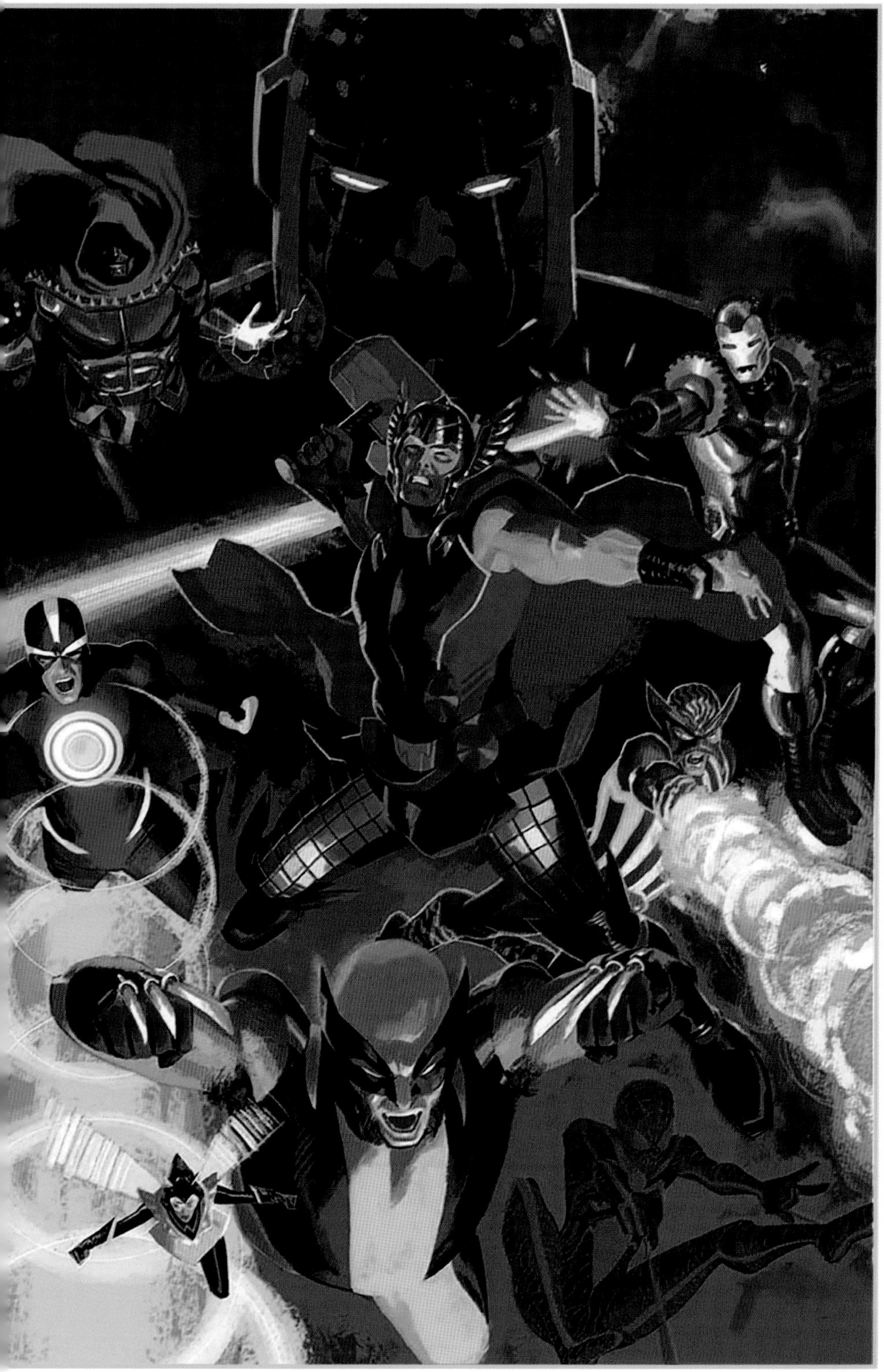

Ant-Man's enemies

Things get tough for Ant-Man when his foes team up. Yellowjacket is a super villain with giant stingers on his suit. He has recruited Crossfire and Egghead as his backup. They all detest Ant-Man because he keeps spoiling their criminal schemes.

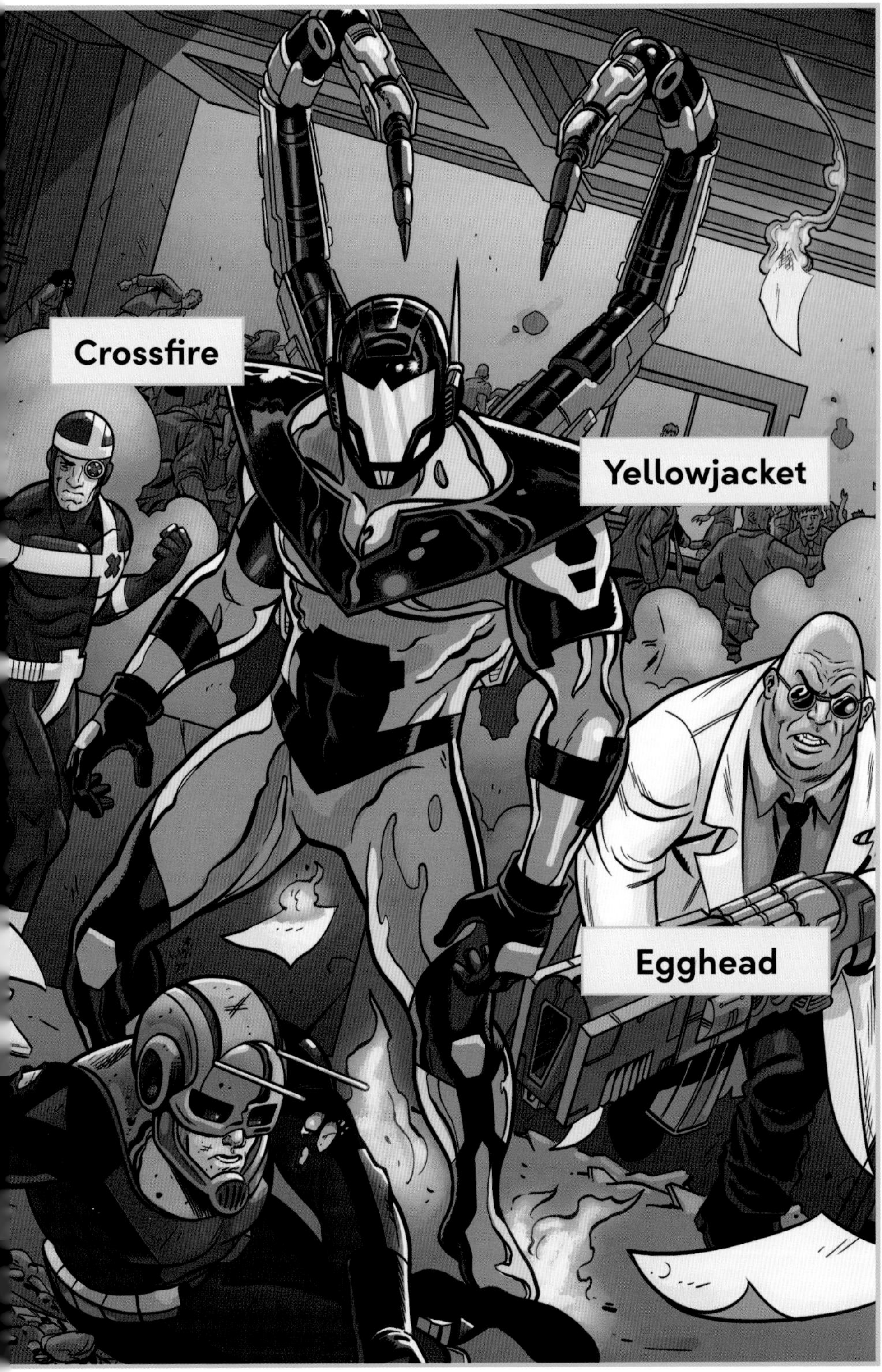
Crossfire
Yellowjacket
Egghead

The Wasp's foes

One of the Wasp's most dangerous foes is Ultron. This giant robot gets stronger and stronger because it keeps upgrading itself. Ultron wants to get rid of Super Heroes and take over the world.

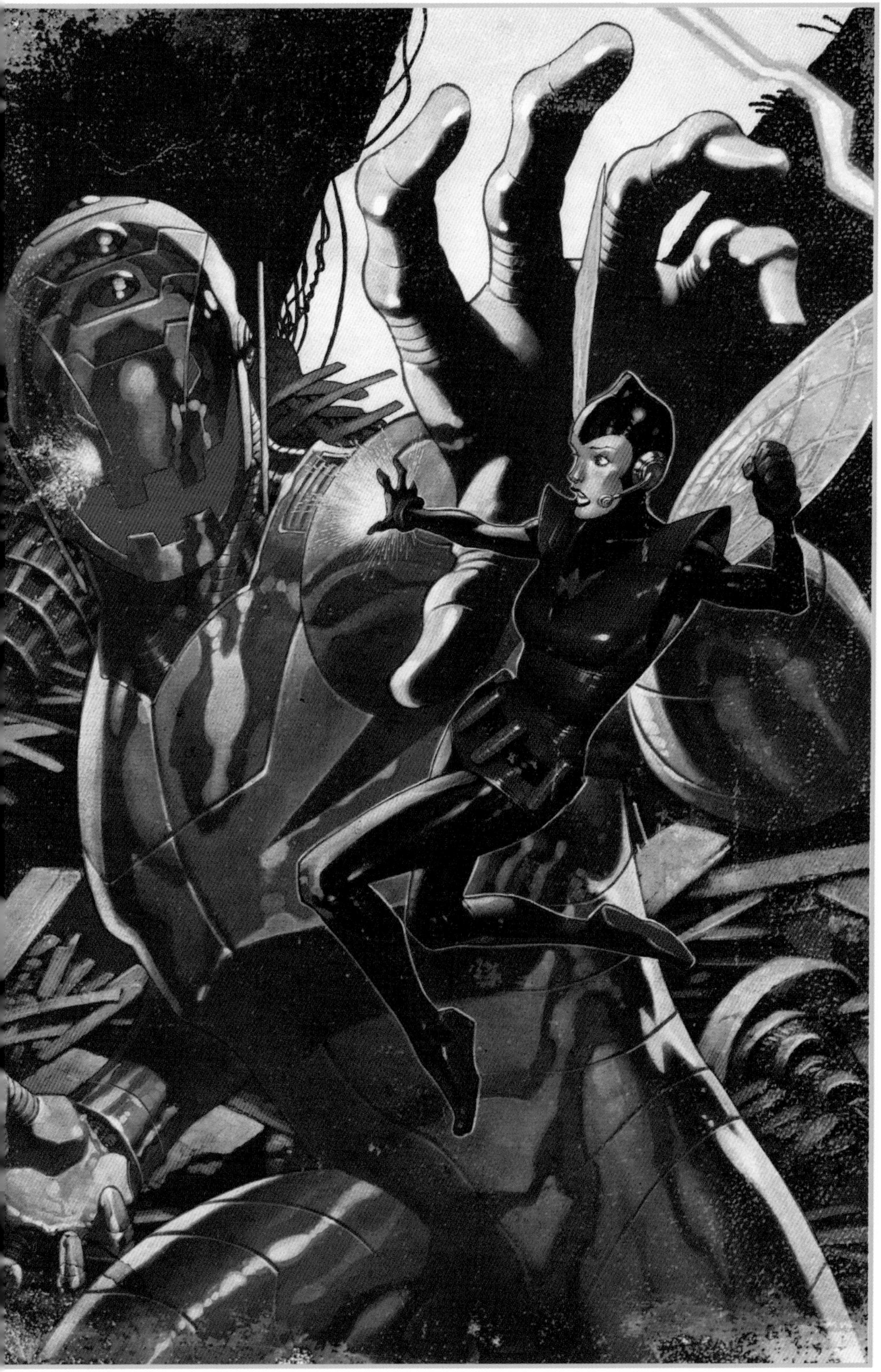

Saving the day

Ant-Man and the Wasp became Super Heroes to fight villains on Earth. Now they fight villains all over the Universe. Wherever their adventures take them, they always save the day. They are proof that small heroes really can make a big impact!

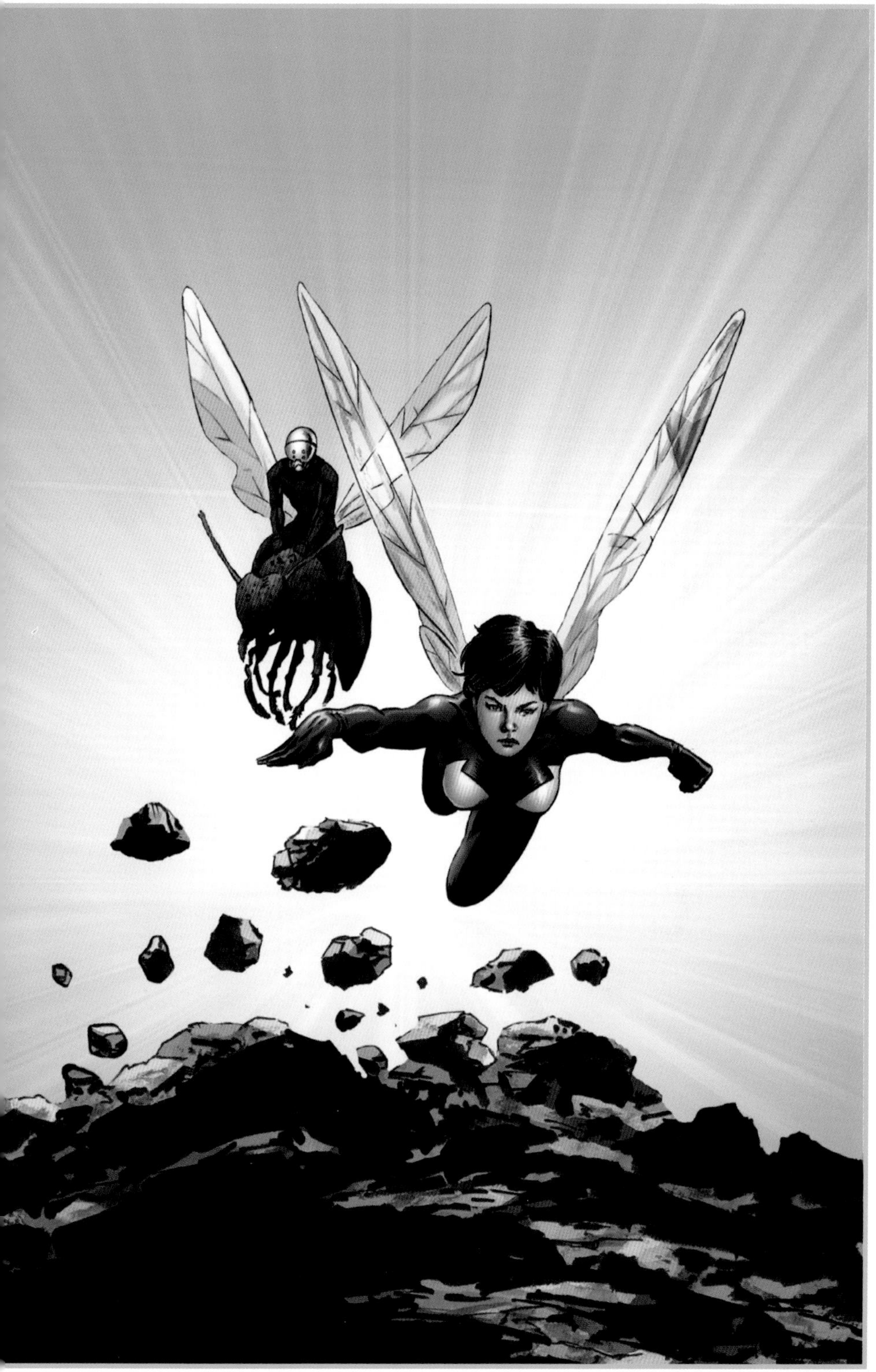

Glossary

antennas
metal bars that send
and receive signals

combine
to join together

contract
to become smaller

criminal
someone who does something
that is against the law

detest
to strongly dislike

electronics engineer
someone who designs things that
are powered by electricity

expand
to become bigger

harmony
getting along together peacefully

mutant
someone who is born
with superpowers

particles
tiny little pieces of something

role model
a person you admire and
want to be like

save the day
to prevent something bad
from happening

Index

Quiz

What have you learned about Ant-Man and the Wasp?

1. What job did Scott Lang do before he became Ant-Man?

2. What does G.I.R.L. stand for?

3. Who was the first Ant-Man?

4. Which Super Hero team have Ant-Man and the Wasp both been in?

5. Where does the Wasp wear her stingers?

6. What is the name of the giant robot that wants to get rid of Super Heroes?

7. Pym Particles enable Ant-Man and the Wasp to shrink or grow. True or false?

1. Electrical engineer 2. Geniuses In action Research Labs 3. Hank Pym 4. The Avengers 5. On her wrists 6. Ultron 7. True